Ghastly Public Library

Ghastly Gourmand

Bank of Ghastly

Ghastly Antiques

43 Old Cemetery Road:
Book Three

TILL DEATH DO US BARK

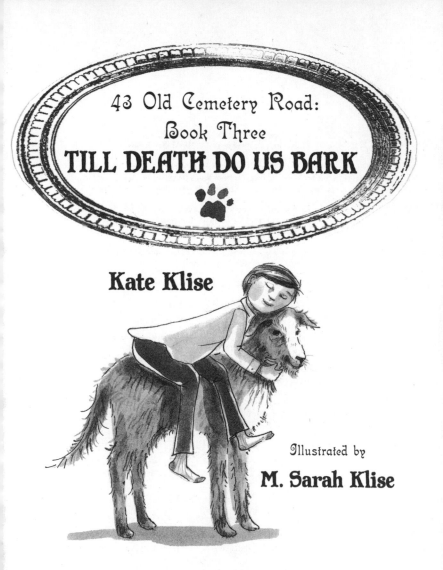

Kate Klise

Illustrated by

M. Sarah Klise

Harcourt
Houghton Mifflin Harcourt
BOSTON   NEW YORK   2011

Harcourt Children's Books is an imprint of Houghton Mifflin Harcourt
Publishing Company.

www.hmhbooks.com

Library of Congress Cataloging-in-Publication Data

Klise, Kate.
Till death do us bark / written by Kate Klise ; illustrated by M. Sarah Klise.
p. cm. — (43 Old Cemetery Road ; bk. 3)
Summary: In this story told mostly through letters, Noah Breth's feuding children
come to Ghastly, Illinois, to follow a trail of limericks to their inheritance, while
Seymour tries to convince Iggy and Olive to let him keep Mr. Breth's dog.
ISBN 978-0-547-40036-5
[1. Inheritance and succession—Fiction. 2. Coins—Fiction. 3. Dogs—Fiction. 4. Ghosts—Fiction.
5. Haunted houses—Fiction. 6. Authors—Fiction. 7. Letters—Fiction. 8. Humorous stories.]
I. Klise, M. Sarah, ill. II. Title.
PZ7.K684Til 2011
[Fic] —dc22
2010009065

Designed by M. Sarah Klise

Manufactured in USA
DOC 10 9 8 7 6 5 4 3 2 1
4500281170

That man is the richest whose pleasures are the cheapest.

Henry David Thoreau

And this is me, Seymour.
I'm an artist.
I'm illustrating a book Mr. Grumply and Olive are writing. It's called 43 Old Cemetery Road. We named it after the address of our house. We publish three chapters at a time and send them to readers all over the world.
Did I mention 43 Old Cemetery Road is already an international bestseller?
Not long ago Olive and Mr. Grumply adopted me. It was the happiest day of my life!
(My other parents are in jail, which is fine with me.)

That's the story you're going to read now.
It all began with the most innocent question in the world:

Can I have a dog?

☐ Yes

☐ No

☐ Maybe

43 Old Cemetery Road
Third Floor
Ghastly, Illinois

November 3

Dear Olive and Mr. Grumply,

A dog followed me home from the library today. I've always wanted a dog, and this one has a lot of personality. He even smiles!

Can I keep him? I promise to take good care of him.

Please say YES!

    —Seymour

P.S. Do I have to keep writing letters? Can't we just talk, like a normal family?

November 3

Dear Seymour and Iggy,

I don't know how Iggy feels about dogs, but I feel strongly. I was a cat person all my life. Now I guess you could call me a cat ghost. I simply adore the elegance and sophistication of *Felis catus.*

I suppose it wouldn't kill me to try to befriend a dog. But I'm concerned about Shadow. Our cat might not take kindly to a canine creature. Is there perhaps a better home for this dog—one without a resident cat? What do you think, Iggy?

As for writing letters, I insist upon it. Letter writing has become a dying art. If we don't keep it alive, who will?

Love,

Olive

IGNATIUS B. GRUMPLY

A WRITER IN RESIDENCE

November 3

Dear Olive and Seymour,

I've always been a dog person myself   mainly because I'm allergic to cats. So I'm less concerned about a cat's hurt feelings than I am about the rightful owner of this dog.

Seymour, have you checked to see if there's a collar on the dog? If so, you must return the dog to the owner listed on the dog tags. If there are no tags, I still want you to make every effort to find the dog's owner. After you've done that, we'll discuss the matter further.

I agree with Olive about the wisdom of communicating via letters. Writers need quiet. That's why I disconnected phone service to Spence Mansion when I moved in. With three new chapters of our book due to readers by Thanksgiving, we need all the quiet we can get.

Resting and writing in peace,

Ignatius

Ignatius

➤THE GHASTLY TIMES◄

Tuesday, November 4
Cliff Hanger, Editor

"Your Secrets Are Our Business"

50 Cents
Morning Edition

Is This Your Dog?

Seymour Hope is seeking information regarding a large dog that followed him home from the Ghastly Public Library yesterday.

"I'll take care of him if nobody wants him," offered Hope, age 11. "Most folks probably wouldn't want a dog this big and slobbery."

The animal wears a collar with two small tags. "One of the tags is old and dirty," said Hope. "But the other tag is engraved with the word 'Secret.' I bet that's the dog's name."

Seymour Hope lives at 43 Old Cemetery Rd. with Ignatius B. Grumply and the ghost of Olive C. Spence. Grumply and Spence recently adopted the boy, who was abandoned by his parents in May.

Seymour Hope is looking for the owner of this dog.

Noah Breth: Dead at Age 95

Noah Breth, Ghastly's beloved multi-millionaire, died yesterday. He was 95 years old.

Born in Ireland in 1913, Breth moved to the United States as a young man. He met and married Sweetie Pye. The couple raised two children in their Ghastly home, known locally as the Old Breth Place.

Noah Breth was an avid collector of antiques, artwork and rare books.

"Mr. Breth had one of the finest collections in the country," said Mac Awbrah, owner of Ghastly Antiques. "But even more impressive was his generous spirit and robust sense of humor."

Noah Breth was preceded in death by his wife, Sweetie, who died 22 years ago at home. He is survived by his grown children, Kitty and Kanine. Neither has visited Ghastly much in recent years.

By his request, there will be no funeral or memorial service for Noah Breth. According to his lawyer, Rita O'Bitt, Breth requested that "no

Breth was known for his wit and wealth.

(Continued on page 2, column 1)

BRETH *(Continued from page 1, column 2)*

fuss" be made of his passing. "Mr. Breth told me if people wanted to do something to remember him, they should do whatever makes them smile," said O'Bitt.

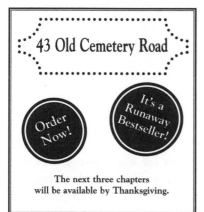
Penny for Your Thoughts

M. Balm says old coin was discovered

M. Balm, chief librarian at the Ghastly Public Library, often finds old pennies in the library's late fees box.

But it's not often he finds a 1909 penny.

"I found it yesterday at the very bottom of the box," said Balm. "I almost took it to the bank with the rest of the coins, but I'm glad I didn't. It could be worth something. Just like old librarians, old coins are often more valuable than they appear at face value."

Balm says he doesn't know who put the penny in the box. "We collect late fees on an honor system," he explained. "People returning overdue books simply drop bills or coins in the box. So I have no idea whose penny this was."

Nor does Balm know how much the penny is worth. "But I'll find out," he said. "I work in a library!"

Kitty Breth

4 Cheshire Court   Cat Creek, Montana

November 5

Rita O'Bitt
Attorney-at-Law
95 Coffin Avenue
Ghastly, Illinois

Dear Ms. O'Bitt,

I know that you were Daddy's lawyer for many years, so I'm
assuming that you have a copy of his will. May I also assume
that Daddy told you I was his favorite child? He couldn't stand
my brother, Kanine, any more than I can. If Kanine calls or
writes to you, tell him to keep his paws off Daddy's money!

I'll arrive in Ghastly tomorrow. Let's get together as soon as
possible to discuss how best to transfer Daddy's assets to my
bank account. You can write to me at Daddy's house. I'll be
staying there rather than at the Ghastly Inn. I want to avoid
any close encounters of the Kanine kind.

Sincerely,

Kitty Breth

Kitty Breth

P.S. Here's a picture of Daddy and me.

KANINE BRETH

478 Fetch Boulevard
Dog Island, Florida

November 5

Rita O'Bitt
Attorney-at-Law
95 Coffin Avenue
Ghastly, Illinois

Dear Ms. O'Bitt,

I will arrive in Ghastly tomorrow to settle my father's estate. I'd like to set up a time to come to your office and discuss my father's will. I'm sure you have it.

I'm afraid it won't be pretty when my sister finds out that Dad left everything to me. Kitty's been trying to get her claws into Dad's money for years. But isn't it obvious from this picture that **I** was his favorite?

The truth is, Kitty and Dad were never very close. How can you be close to someone who lies, cheats, and steals? And those are Kitty's **GOOD** qualities. If she contacts you, be careful. (Just saying.)

Sincerely,

Kanine Breth

Kanine Breth

P.S. You can write to me at the Old Breth Place. I plan to stay there while in town.

RITA O'BITT

ATTORNEY-AT-LAW
95 COFFIN AVENUE
GHASTLY, ILLINOIS

November 7

Kitty and Kanine Breth
The Old Breth Place
Rt. 1, Box 257
Ghastly, Illinois

Dear Kitty and Kanine,

I'm very sorry for your loss. As you know, I represented your father for many years. He was a truly fascinating man and a delightful client. Noah brought a smile to the face of everyone he met.

The only difficult thing your father ever asked me to do was help him prepare his last will and testament. I agreed, but reluctantly. It's a rather unique document, as you'll discover. But the will is legal—I made sure of that—and clearly states where Noah Breth's vast fortune will go now that he is dead.

In accordance with his wishes, I will rèad your father's will to you at nine o'clock on the morning of November 23, exactly twenty days after the date of his death.

Until then, I am enclosing a sealed envelope from your father. Please open it and read his words carefully.

Sincerely,

Rita O'Bitt

Rita O'Bitt

P.S. Almost forgot: It seems your dad's dog has wandered over to Spence Mansion. I saw Secret's picture in the paper. A boy named Seymour is taking care of the dog. I'll talk to Seymour and let him know he can return Secret to the Old Breth Place. Or if you prefer, you can retrieve the dog at your earliest convenience. The address of Spence Mansion is 43 Old Cemetery Road.

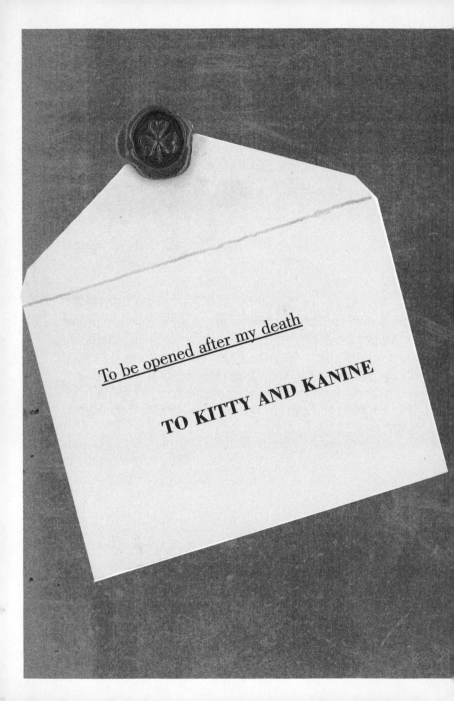

NOAH BRETH

November 1

Dear Kitty and Kanine,

When you read this letter, I'll be dead. A strange thing to imagine! But I can't complain.

I enjoyed a full life. I had a happy marriage. I found satisfying work as a collector. And I had two children who spent their lives fighting.

It is my one regret that I could do nothing about your incessant squabbling during my lifetime. And so in death I am determined to do otherwise.

My collection of artwork, antiques, and rare books was recently appraised at seven million dollars. My millions can be yours to share with each other or to keep for yourself. All you have to do is solve a simple riddle.

There are no directions or instructions, other than these few lines:

> There once was a rich man who said,
> While lying upon his deathbed:
> "I'm really too ill
> To write my last will."
> So he wrote some verses instead.

And as he grew closer to dyin'
He knew he oughta be cryin'
'Cause his family tree
Was down to just three
But his kids weren't there for good-byein'.

And that's when this very rich man
Decided he needed a plan
To make *sense* of his wealth
While still in good health.
Now go find it all if you can!

Sincerely yours, Dad

P.S. Are you befuddled? All right, I'll give you a wee hint. I hid my fortune in what I treasured most on earth.

P.P.S. This is the last letter you'll ever receive from me. I don't expect to hear back. You kids never did write to me, except when you needed money or wanted to badmouth each other. Pity I was unsuccessful in sharing with you the joys of writing a nice letter.

November 8

Rita O'Bitt
Attorney-at-Law
95 Coffin Avenue
Ghastly, Illinois

Dear Ms. O'Bitt,

I know you're busy helping the Breths settle their father's estate. But I have a question of some urgency that I hope you can answer.

Did you hear about the 1909 penny I found? I did a little research and found out it's called a wheat penny because of the two wheat stalks on the back of the coin, also known as the reverse. The front of the coin, or the obverse, features a profile of Abraham Lincoln.

When President Theodore
Roosevelt wanted a new penny
designed to commemorate the
one hundredth birthday of
Abraham Lincoln in 1909, he
chose the artist Victor David
Brenner, an immigrant from
Lithuania who had made a
name for himself as a sculptor.

Victor David Brenner
(1871–1924)

Well, everyone loved the
way Brenner depicted
Abraham Lincoln on the
front of the new coin. But
the reverse side infuriated
many people. Why?
Because there, at the very
bottom, Brenner had in-
cluded his initials, "V.D.B."

People were outraged! In fairness to Mr. Brenner, coin
designers in other countries often included their entire
names on coins. But criticism in this country was so
intense that only 484,000 coins were minted in 1909 in
San Francisco—that's what the tiny "S" means on the
front—before the U.S. Mint was forced to remove Mr.
Brenner's initials.

Attitudes changed, however, and by 1918, Brenner's initials were restored to the coin but moved to the front. If
you look closely at a penny today, you'll see "V.D.B." in

teeny tiny letters on the bottom of Lincoln's coat. You'll also likely see the Lincoln Memorial on the other side. This image replaced the wheat stalks in 1959.

I hope you're still reading because my point in telling you all this is simple: The 1909-S V.D.B. penny I found is worth $8,500!

Should I turn the coin over to the police so they can try to return it to the person who put it in the late fees box? Or would it be okay for me to claim this coin is now the property of the library? We could certainly use the money to buy new books.

I would appreciate your professional opinion—or should I say, your *two cents'* worth?

Sincerely,

M. Balm

M. Balm

P.S. Isn't that Noah Breth's dog over at Spence Mansion? I can hear him barking from here!

RITA O'BITT

ATTORNEY-AT-LAW
95 COFFIN AVENUE
GHASTLY, ILLINOIS

November 10

M. Balm
Ghastly Public Library
12 Scary Street
Ghastly, Illinois

Dear Mr. Balm,

Who knew the humble penny had such an interesting history? Thank you for sharing your research with me.

In exchange I'm pleased to tell you that the 1909 penny became the property of the library as soon as it was placed in the late fees box. Happy book buying!

Oh, and thank you for reminding me about Mr. Breth's dog. I meant to contact Seymour Hope the day I saw Secret's picture in the newspaper, but forgot. I'm going to take a walk over to Spence Mansion right now and talk to the boy.

Yours sincerely,

Rita O'Bitt

43 Old Cemetery Road
Third Floor
Ghastly, Illinois

November 10

HAND-DELIVERED

Ms. Rita O'Bitt
Attorney-at-Law
95 Coffin Avenue
Ghastly, Illinois

Dear Ms. O'Bitt,

I'm sorry I didn't invite you inside the house. And I'm
doubly sorry for interrupting when you started to tell
me that Secret was Noah Breth's dog. I didn't want
Olive or Mr. Grumply to hear you.

I know Secret belonged to Mr. Breth. Several people have told me. But Mr. Breth is dead, and dead people can't take care of dogs. I'm alive and I promise I'm taking really good care of Secret. We play fetch every day. I'm teaching him how to sit and roll over. Sometimes he even lets me ride him. If you don't count his barking, he's really a great dog.

I don't think it's hurting anybody for Secret to live here. Do you?

Sincerely,

    —Seymour Hope

P.S. Please don't tell Olive or Mr. Grumply that we talked about this.

RITA O'BITT

ATTORNEY-AT-LAW
95 COFFIN AVENUE
GHASTLY, ILLINOIS

November 10

Seymour Hope
Third floor
43 Old Cemetery Road
Ghastly, Illinois

Dear Seymour,

I suppose if you're willing to keep Secret, I can keep
a secret, too—especially with a boy who knows how
to write a nice letter.

Sincerely,

Rita O'Bitt

SEYMOUR HOPE
Illustrator in Residence

43 Old Cemetery Road
Third Floor
Ghastly, Illinois

November 11

Dear Olive and Mr. Grumply,

It's been a week since Secret's picture was in the paper, and no one has come to claim him. So can I keep him? You could write the next three chapters about Secret. Please think about it. I could draw pictures of Secret all day long.

Love,

—Seymour and Secret

-Seymour

IGNATIUS B. GRUMPLY

A WRITER IN RESIDENCE

43 OLD CEMETERY ROAD   **2ND FLOOR**   **GHASTLY, ILLINOIS**

November 11

Olive C. Spence
The Cupola
43 Old Cemetery Road
Ghastly, Illinois

Dear Olive,

Since I can't sleep, I might as well write. What do you think of Seymour's request? I tend to think th

Hello, darling.

Olive! You startled me. So you're awake, too.

Who can sleep with that beast barking outside? It's loud enough to wake the dead.

A terrible distraction, yes. But not as bad as your friend.

What do you mean, dear?

Shadow. The cat. My allergies have never been worse. You don't suppose Shadow's invited some feline friends to move in with us, do you?

No, Iggy. We have just one cat, and I've not seen

the poor thing for days. That insufferable dog must've scared him off. Is it possible you're allergic to Secret?

Not a chance. I had a golden retriever my entire childhood. That dog was my best friend for many years. Caring for him taught me a lot about responsibility. You have to admit, Olive, there's nothing quite like a dog as a pet.

I'll admit nothing of the kind. Cats are infinitely superior. They're graceful and elegant. Independent, too. And unlike dogs, cats don't keep the neighborhood up all night with their boorish barking.

True. But dogs don't skulk around like cats.

What on earth are you talking about?

Cats have a sneaky way of slinking and skulking that, frankly, I find a bit unsettling.

I take grave exception to that. And wipe your nose! It's dripping.

Forgive me. It's these blasted allergies.

Perhaps you should see a doctor.

I will—as soon as we finish these next three chapters. What do you think of Seymour's idea that we base the next installment of our book on Secret?

I prefer cat stories. Besides, Secret belongs at the Old Breth Place. That dog was Noah Breth's faithful companion.

Is this true? How do you know?

Oh, Iggy, if you'd learn the gentle art of eaves-dropping, you'd be a far wiser man.

Maybe. But if the dog has a home, Seymour needs to return him. Or am I missing something here?

What you're missing is a simple fact: This is the first time Seymour has ever kept a secret from me.

Wait. Seymour *knows* that Secret was Noah Breth's dog?

Yes. Several people have told him so, including Rita O'Bitt. She was here yesterday afternoon.

Then it sounds to me like Seymour hasn't been honest with us. If he's lying, he needs to be punished.

I disagree. A secret isn't a lie.

What's the difference?

A secret is simply a decision to withhold certain truths, whereas a lie is an outright misstatement of fact. Seymour hasn't lied to us. He said that no one has come to claim the dog. And techni-cally, that's true.

I don't like it. It's not honest. It's sneaky and skulky like a ca

Don't you dare use the word "cat" in a pejorative context!

I'll use whatever I like. And I'll punish Seymour if he needs to be punished.

Oh, you dog people are all alike.

What's *that* supposed to mean?

You think you can train a child like a dog. Don't you realize the threat of punishment only serves to turn children into better liars?

So your approach is to let Seymour sneak around and deceive us? We're his parents now, Olive. We have a responsibility to give praise when appropriate and disci-pline when necessary.

I agree. I just don't think children should be treated like dogs. We can let Seymour make his own choices and, if necessary, suffer the conse-quences like an adult.

But he's not an adult.

He's certainly not a dog!

I didn't say he was.

Don't write to me in that tone. It's the equiva-lent of shouting.

I'm not SHOUTING. I'm simply trying to make a point. I believe I know how modern children should be trained.

Is that so? You didn't even know Seymour was keeping a secret. Who has more experience with the boy? I've known him since the day he was born.

Oh, yeah? Well, I've BEEN a boy since the day *I* was BORN!

I refuse to continue this conversation if you're going to raise your font at me.

Olive, don't go. Please! We have to discuss the next three chapters of the book. They're due in just sixteen days.

Sorry. Must slink away now.

THE GHASTLY TIMES

Wednesday, November 12
Cliff Hanger, Editor

"Your Secrets Are Our Business"

50 Cents
Afternoon Edition

Is His Bark Worse Than His Bite?

Anyone within a half mile of Spence Mansion could hear it.

Secret, the dog that followed Seymour Hope home from the library last week, hasn't bitten anyone.

"But he barks from dusk till dawn," said M. Balm. "I hate to complain, but I haven't slept a wink all week."

Hope apologized for the inconvenience. "I'm trying to keep Secret quiet. I really am. He's my dog now because no one has come to claim him."

Not quite, according to his father.

"I told Seymour that as soon as I finish writing the next three chapters of our book, he and I would have a man-to-man talk," said Ignatius B. Grumply.

Fay Tality has a different version of events. "Grumply didn't exactly tell Seymour that," tattled Tality. "He yelled it.

Secret's not the only one barking at Spence Mansion.

I could hear Ignatius barking and sneezing all the way from my house!"

Grumply is highly allergic to cat dander.

Check Your Pockets!
Another Valuable Coin Found

Shirley is surely happy about the coin she found.

A rare and valuable coin was found this morning at the bottom of a local tip jar.

"It's a two-cent piece from 1872," said Ghastly Gourmand owner Shirley U. Jest. "Goodness knows how long it's been there."

Surely not since 1872. Jest says she empties the tip jar every week.

"Most people stick a dollar or two in the tip jar," she said. "I'm usually not too excited about seeing small change, but this two-cent piece is lovely. I've never seen anything like it!"

(Continued on page 2, column 1)

POCKETS *(Continued from page 1, column 2)*

Neither had M. Balm, chief librarian at the Ghastly Public Library. But after finding a 1909 penny in the late fees box last week, Balm ordered several books on coin collecting.

"It turns out the 1909 penny, which I should note is the legal property of the Ghastly Public Library, is worth $8,500," said Balm. "And Shirley's two-cent piece is worth $10,000."

Surely he jests. "Not at all," said Balm. "It's true!"

Noah Breth's Children Arrive in Ghastly

Kitty and Kanine Breth arrived in Ghastly last week. The siblings are in town to settle the estate of their father, the late Noah Breth.

"I thought my brother would stay at the Ghastly Inn," said Kitty Breth. "But it turns out he was at our old house when I arrived. Ugh, he really is the bad Breth."

"Don't believe a word my sister says," countered Kanine Breth. "And watch your wallets and purses, folks. When it comes to money, Kitty is no pussycat."

It's unclear how Breth's fortune will be divided between his children. According to Rita O'Bitt, Breth asked that his last will and testament be read 20 days after his death, which would be November 23.

"Until then, Daddy left us some silly limericks to read," said Kitty Breth. "We all know what a quirky sense of humor Daddy had. If I were Kanine, I'd ignore the poems completely."

Kitty claims Kanine is the bad Breth while Kanine insists Kitty is no pussycat.

Kitty Breth

Temporary Address

Route 1, Box 257
Ghastly, Illinois

November 12

Mr. Mac Awbrah
Proprietor, Ghastly Antiques
2 Scary Street
Ghastly, Illinois

Dear Mr. Awbrah,

It is IMPERATIVE that I see you as soon as possible to discuss my father's collection. As I'm sure you know, there's nothing on earth Daddy treasured more than his antiques and artwork.

That's why I was surprised to arrive at Daddy's house and find those things missing. My hunch is that he hid his most valuable assets in storage somewhere for safekeeping. Do you know where?

As soon as I can find Daddy's treasures, I'd like you to give me a full and honest appraisal of their worth. Perhaps you could even help me sell the collection. I'd be willing to pay you a small commission for your help.

Sincerely,

Kitty Breth

Kitty Breth

P.S. No need to be in touch with my brother on this matter. Finders keepers is my policy!

November 13

Ms. Kitty Breth
Rt. 1, Box 257
Ghastly, Illinois

GHASTLY ANTIQUES
2 Scary Street
Ghastly, Illinois

Dear Ms. Breth,

I know all about your father's collection. I recently helped him sell his antiques and artwork at Sotheby's. I told your brother the same thing when he called an hour ago.

Your father and I had a wonderful trip to New York. I'm surprised he didn't tell you about it. In any case, I'll attach a few photos so you can see what fun we had at the auction.

I hope you enjoy your stay in Ghastly. And thanks for offering a small commission for my help. No need. Noah offered me a rather large commission, but I refused it. As I told him, it was my pleasure to spend time with a man so kind and generous. I was proud to be his friend.

Antiquatedly yours,

Mac Awbrah

Mac Awbrah

Here we are
at the auction.

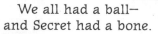

We all had a ball—
and Secret had a bone.

Noah and I
enjoyed a nice
dinner, too.

P.S. Your father wanted me to pass along this envelope
to whichever child wrote a letter to me first asking
about his treasures.

<u>To be opened after my death</u>

TO KITTY OR KANINE

Dear child, have you really not heard
The value that rests in the word?
I suggest that you look
In the home of a book.
Ask the bloke who resembles a bird.

KANINE BRETH

For now:
Rt. 1, Box 257
Ghastly, Illinois

November 14

M. Balm
Ghastly Public Library
12 Scary Street
Ghastly, Illinois

Dear Mr. Balm,

I admit I just opened my sister's mail—but only because she's doing **everything** in her power to cheat me out of my father's money.

Never mind that. You probably know that my father recently died. And I have a sneaking suspicion—based on a little poem I just read—that he might've hidden a lot of money between the pages of a book. It makes sense. My dad valued his collection of rare books even more than his antiques and artwork.

The odd thing is, I can't find any books in his house. So I'm guessing he might've stashed the money between the pages of a library book.

I hope you can help me in this matter. I'm asking you because—well, I hate to tell you this but—you're the bloke in town who most resembles a bird.

Sincerely,

Kanine Breth

Kanine Breth

P.S. If my sister contacts you, ignore her!

41.

GHASTLY PUBLIC LIBRARY

12 Scary Street............................Ghastly, Illinois

M. Balm..Chief Librarian

November 15

Kanine Breth
c/o The Old Breth Place
Rt. 1, Box 257
Ghastly, Illinois

Dear Kanine,

Of course I'm the person your father was referring to! He called me the Word Bird because of my love of reading and my beak-like nose.

Your father was a true friend of the library. Just last month he donated all of his rare books to the library. His collection was valued at more than half a million dollars! We had a grand celebration. (See attached pictures.)

I hope you'll come by the library soon and see the room we've named after your father. What a wonderful man he was! You must be so proud to be his son.

Yours in the written word,

M.Balm

M. Balm

P.S. Your father asked that I pass along the enclosed note to whichever child of his contacted me first by letter.

42.

To be opened after my death

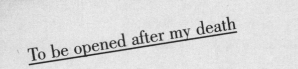

TO KITTY OR KANINE

O my dear daughter or sonny,
I hope that you're finding this funny!
While I love a good book,
For cash you must look
Where the rich stash all of their money.

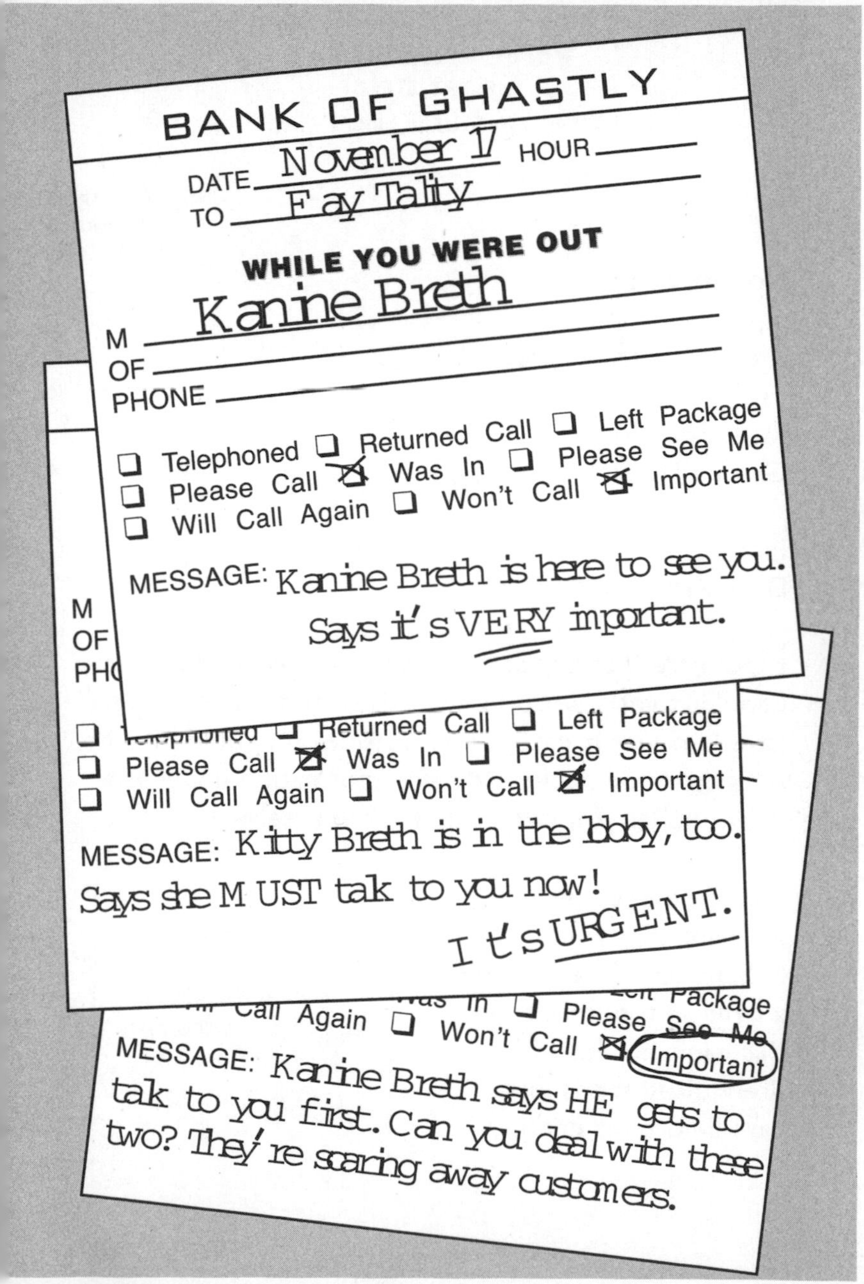
BANK OF GHASTLY
DATE November 17 HOUR
TO Fay Tality
WHILE YOU WERE OUT
M Kanine Breth
OF
PHONE
Telephoned
Returned Call
Left Package
Please Call
Was In
Please See Me
Will Call Again
Won't Call
Important
MESSAGE: Kanine Breth is here to see you. Says it's VERY important.
M
OF
PHO
Returned Call
Left Package
Please Call
Was In
Please See Me
Will Call Again
Won't Call
Important
MESSAGE: Kitty Breth is in the lobby, too. Says she MUST talk to you now! It's URGENT.
Package
Call Again
Won't Call
Please See Me
Important
MESSAGE: Kanine Breth says HE gets to talk to you first. Can you deal with these two? They're scaring away customers.

BANK OF GHASTLY

6 SCARY STREET
GHASTLY, ILLINOIS

Fay Tality
President

November 17

Kitty and Kanine Breth
The Old Breth Place
Rt. 1, Box 257
Ghastly, Illinois

Dear Kitty and Kanine,

I apologize if calling security appeared rude. But when I couldn't get a word in edgewise, I thought it best to have our guards escort you outside so I could put the facts down on paper, slide the information under the door, and let you two read it for yourselves.

You are correct in believing that your father recently deposited a large sum of money in this bank. But he withdrew those funds just days before his death.

Bank of Ghastly

account #5551913
$6,423,500 withdrawn
Account closed on

NOV 01

I'm afraid I can't tell you much more than that. It's none of my business what customers do with their money.

But I can tell you this: Your father was the most beloved customer we ever had. He always had a smile on his face and a kind word for everyone he met.

I'm sorry I couldn't be more helpful. Perhaps you should contact your father's lawyer.

Sincerely,

Fay Tality

KANINE BRETH

Rt. 1, Box 257
Ghastly, Illinois

November 18

Rita O'Bitt
Attorney-at-Law
95 Coffin Avenue
Ghastly, Illinois

Dear Ms. O'Bitt:

I have a bone to pick with you.

How **dare** you let my father sell all of his antiques and artwork and give his rare books to the library! His treasures are **gone**, his bank account is **empty**, and I have **no idea what he did with the money**. He might've thrown it into the wind for all I know!

If you don't tell me where his money is **IMMEDIATELY**, I will sue you for legal malpractice.

Sincerely,

Kanine Breth

Kanine Breth

Temporary Address

Route 1, Box 257
Ghastly, Illinois

November 18

Rita O'Bitt
Attorney-at-Law
95 Coffin Avenue
Ghastly, Illinois

Dear Ms. O'Bitt,

Everything my brother writes is a lie, including the words *Dear* and *Sincerely*. But I agree with him on one point: What kind of lawyer would let an old man withdraw all his money from the bank? You had a responsibility to protect Daddy from people like Kanine who would try to get their grubby paws on Daddy's money, wherever it is.

If Kanine gets to sue you, then I get to sue you, too. And I want to sue Kanine for reading my mail. He did it first! But before that, I demand to know: <u>Where is Daddy's money?</u>

Very sincerely,

Kitty Breth

Kitty Breth

RITA O'BITT

ATTORNEY-AT-LAW
95 COFFIN AVENUE
GHASTLY, ILLINOIS

November 19

Kitty and Kanine Breth
The Old Breth Place
Rt. 1, Box 257
Ghastly, Illinois

Dear Kitty and Kanine,

Your father knew you well. He was fully aware that you did not share his love of antiques, artwork, and rare books. That's why he did you the favor of divesting himself of them shortly before his death.

He asked me to share these particulars with you:

Accounting of the Dispersal of Certain Assets Belonging to Noah Breth

Description	Value	Where are they now?
Rare books	$576,500	Donated to Ghastly Public Library
Antiques & Artwork	$6,423,500	Sold at auction for cash

Total $7,000,000

As for the question of where your father's money is now, please check tomorrow's special at The Ghastly Gourmand for his response.

Sincerely,

Rita O'Bitt

Rita O'Bitt

Welcome to

The Ghastly Gourmand

A Ghastly Favorite for 75 Years

MENU

SANDWICHES

Grilled cheese............$1.50
Meatloaf sandwich............$1.99
Tuna melt............$1.99
PB&J............$1.35
Hot dog............$1.35
Hamburger............$2.15
Cheeseburger............$2.35

OMELETS

Plain............$2.25
Cheese............$2.35
Ham and cheese............$2.75
Mushroom............$2.35
Veggie............$2.35
Potato............$2.35
Spinach and feta............$2.40

November special

Pumpkin muffin: $.75
Add cream cheese: $.25 extra

This week's soup

Creamy butternut squash
Bowl: $1.25   Cup: $.75

SIDES

Chips..........$.50
French fries...........$.75
Cole slaw..........$.65
Baked beans..........$.75
House salad...........$.75

TODAY'S SPECIAL:

There's nothing on earth I deplore
Like fighting over money—oh bore!
So mine now jingles,
Whene'er it mingles.
Now do you know what to look for?

DESSERTS
Brownie............$.75
Ice cream............$.80
Lemon square............$.80
Apple pie............$.95
Chocolate cake............$.95

BEVERAGES
Coffee............$.35
Hot tea............$.35
Iced tea............$.35
Milk............$.50
Chocolate milk............$.60
Lemonade............$.50

Thank you!

Have a Ghastly Day!

⇒THE GHASTLY TIMES⇐

Thursday, November 20
Cliff Hanger, Editor

"Your Secrets Are Our Business"

50 Cents
Afternoon Edition

Noah Joke!
Ghastly Millionaire Put Fortune in Coins

Daily special takes Breths' breath away.

The search is on!

According to a limerick in today's Ghastly Gourmand menu, Noah Breth's fortune is up for grabs.

"How do you like that?" asked Shirley U. Jest, owner of the Ghastly Gourmand. "Mr. Breth put his money in coins. What else jingles whenever it mingles?"

Jest said she received the limerick from Rita O'Bitt. "Noah knew his kids would get

steamed when they couldn't find his millions," explained Jest. "So he wrote that little poem and asked Rita to deliver it to me as soon as the Breth kids threatened to sue her. Ha! Isn't that just the cleverest thing you ever heard?"

Not everyone agreed.

"This is outrageous!" said Kitty Breth moments after reading the limerick. "I intend to talk to the sheriff."

"Not before I do!" barked Kanine Breth.

Ghastly County Sheriff Mike Ondolences said it was unlikely local law enforcement would get involved. "A man has the right to do whatever he wants with his money," said Ondolences. "Seems like old Noah wanted everyone in town to have a chance to get a piece of his fortune. Nothing wrong with that."

Attorney Rita O'Bitt refused to speculate on the rhyme or reason behind Breth's last wishes. "All I can say is that the reading of Mr. Breth's will is scheduled for this Sunday. I trust all questions will be answered then."

Another Rare Coin Discovered in . . . Beans?

A third valuable coin was discovered this morning at Ghastly Grocers.

"It was the strangest thing," says owner Kay Daver. "I was tidying up the produce section when I saw something shiny under a pile of green beans. I picked it up and saw it was a little silver coin."

And not just any silver coin.

"What Kay found was a 1795 half dime," said M. Balm, chief librarian at the Ghastly Public Library. "According to my new books on coin collecting, it's the rare Flowing Hair half dime. It was not a

(Continued on page 2, column 1)

BEANS *(Continued from page 1, column 2)*

popular design because many people didn't like the messy hair on the front of the coin or the skinny eagle on the back. This design was discontinued after only two years. As a result it's worth $25,000 today."

"Cool beans!" said Daver, who added that Noah Breth had been a regular shopper at Ghastly Grocers. "He must've hidden the coin under the beans before he died."

Balm said he now believes it was Noah Breth who slipped the 1909 penny in the library late fees box and the 1872 two-cent piece in the tip jar at the Ghastly Gourmand.

Daver delights in half dime.

Till Death Do Us Bark

The nocturnal noises from Spence Mansion continue to keep much of Ghastly awake.

"I'm not sure whose barking is worse," said Fay Tality. "Ignatius is louder, but Secret barks all night long."

Ignatius Grumply apologized for the noise. "I'm under a great deal of stress," he explained. "We've promised our readers three new chapters by Thanksgiving. That's a week away. But I've not written a word because of this blasted dog and my wretched ca—ca—catCHOO!"

Grumply added that his cat allergies have never been worse. He plans to get rid of Shadow, the cat, as soon as he can find the feline. And what about Secret?

"I am not a fan of secrets," said Grumply. "Especially big secrets children keep from their parents. I hope Seymour is finally ready to be honest with me after our, um, discussion last night."

"Discussion?" said Tality. "It was more like a verbal concussion."

It's no Secret who the real barker is.

November 20

Seymour Hope
Third floor
43 Old Cemetery Road
Ghastly, Illinois

Dear Seymour,

I'm sorry I lost my temper—again—last night. I don't enjoy shouting. But I don't like to be lied to, either.

Does Secret belong to someone else? Some other family, perhaps? If so, you must return him to his rightful home.

I expect an honest answer from you.

Ignatius

Ignatius

P.S. Have you heard from Olive lately? I'm afraid we're having a bit of a cat fight over a dog.

43 Old Cemetery Road
Third Floor
Ghastly, Illinois

November 20

Dear Mr. Grumply,

Please don't be mad at me. I'm trying to be a good son.
I really am. And here's the truth: Secret doesn't belong
to a living soul—except me.

—Seymour

P.S. I haven't seen Olive lately—or Shadow. I wonder
where they are.

O.C.S.

Ghost Writer in Residence

43 Old Cemetery Road, The Cupola
Ghastly, Illinois

November 20

Dear Seymour,

I'm here. I've been frantically floating around
town, looking for Shadow.

Ignatius has some nerve threatening to get rid of
our cat when the poor thing isn't even here.
Shadow's been scared away from the only place
he's ever called home—by a *dog,* no less. And yet
Ignatius continues to blame his sneezing on
Shadow. The whole thing is maddening!

What do you have to say for yourself, Seymour?

Olive

P.S. I apologize if I sound cranky, but I haven't
had a decent night's sleep since that rag mop of a
dog arrived.

58.

43 Old Cemetery Road
Third Floor
Ghastly, Illinois

November 20

Dear Olive,

I'm sorry Secret's been keeping you up at night.

And disturbing my afternoon naps.

Olive. You're here! I really am sorry. I'm trying to
teach Secret to be quiet. And I'll help you find
Shadow.

I'm not sure Shadow wants to come home if
that dog is still here.

59.

Can't this be Secret's home, too? He's a good dog. If you'd just get to know him a little, I think you'd like him a lot.

Hmm. I don't know about that. But I do know one thing: You're not being honest with me. Does Secret belong here?

If he has an owner, he hasn't contacted me.

I want you to tell me the truth, the whole truth, and nothing but the truth.

I'm trying to.

Sometimes we have to do things we don't like.

I know.

The time has come for you to do that. Do you understand?

Yeah. I think so.

All right, then. You know what must be done.

Can it wait till morning?

Of course. I just want you to do the right thing.

I will.

Thank you, dear. Now good night.

Good night. And good-bye.

MISSING PERSON REPORT

Ghastly Sheriff's Office
Ghastly County Courthouse
16 Scary Street **Ghastly, Illinois**

Name of missing person: ___Seymour Hope___

Last seen:
      Location ___43 Old Cemetery Road___
      Time ___Nov. 20, 10:30 p.m.___

Reported missing by: ___Ignatius B. Grumply___

Did the person leave: voluntarily __x__ involuntarily _____

Did the person take anything from home?
(If so, provide list of items taken.)
___Sleeping bag and pillow, dog biscuits,___
___large dog___

Other information: ___He left a note behind___
_____(See attached) ——————→

Photo:

Report filed by: _Sheriff Mike Ondolences_

SEYMOUR HOPE
Illustrator in Residence

43 Old Cemetery Road
Third Floor
Ghastly, Illinois

November 20

Dear Olive and Mr. Grumply,

I'm sorry for ruining everything. It's my fault Secret barks so much. It's my fault Shadow ran away. It's my fault you two are fighting and not getting any work done on the book.

My old mom and dad used to call me a liar. They didn't believe I had a friend who was a ghost. I hated being called a liar, especially because I was telling the truth.

63.

But now I really am a liar. I didn't want to make you guys mad. But I didn't want to give up Secret, either. I know he doesn't belong to me. But I pretended he did. The only solution I can think of is to run away with Secret. So that's what I'm doing.

I think Shadow will come back once Secret's gone. And you won't miss any more sleep on account of Secret's barking. Best of all, you won't have to live with a liar like me.

Love and good—bye forever,

—Seymour

IGNATIUS B. GRUMPLY

A WRITER IN RESIDENCE

43 OLD CEMETERY ROAD   2ND FLOOR   GHASTLY, ILLINOIS

<u>DELIVERED BY HAND</u>

November 21

Sheriff Mike Ondolences
Ghastly County Courthouse
16 Scary Street
Ghastly, Illinois

Dear Sheriff,

I am beyond distraught about my son. Therefore
I am pleading with you to do everything in your
power to locate Seymour and return him safely
home. Please spare no expense of time or energy.

Yours in crisis,

Ignatius B. Grumply

Ignatius B. Grumply

November 21

Ignatius B. Grumply
43 Old Cemetery Road
Ghastly, Illinois

Mr. Grumply:

A search crew is out right now trying to locate Seymour. Believe me, we are doing everything we can to find your son.

Unfortunately, I also have to deal with distractions like Kitty and Kanine Breth. If you don't believe me, read the enclosed letter.

Yours in the law,

Mike Ondolences

Mike Ondolences

Kitty Breth

Temporary Address

Route 1, Box 257
Ghastly, Illinois

November 20

Sheriff Mike Ondolences
Ghastly County Courthouse
16 Scary Street
Ghastly, Illinois

Dear Sheriff Ondolences,

Nothing gets my dander up like injustice. That's why I'm writing to tell you that I have PROOF my stupid brother is trying to swindle me out of my share of our father's money.

Just take a look at this phone conversation he had with Brad Pitbuhl, the most unscrupulous lawyer money can buy. I recorded them talking on the phone and transcribed the conversation for your convenience.

Yours seeking justice,

Kitty Breth

Kitty Breth

TRANSCRIPT OF TELEPHONE CONVERSATION

KANINE BRETH: Hello?

BRAD PITBUHL: Hey, it's me, Brad Pitbuhl.

KANINE BRETH: About time. What took you so long?

BRAD PITBUHL: I've been researching your case and trying to come up with a strategy.

KANINE BRETH: And?

BRAD PITBUHL: Here's the plan. Forget the local yokels. We'll get the FBI involved. I have connections there. We'll claim the rare coins found around Ghastly are stolen goods.

KANINE BRETH: Stolen? From whom?

BRAD PITBUHL: From you, you dolt! Your father meant to give you those coins, but he died before he was able to. Remember how he told you he had some valuable coins he wanted to give you?

KANINE BRETH: No.

BRAD PITBUHL: Try harder.

KANINE BRETH: I'm trying to remember, but I can't because he never . . . Oh, wait a minute. I get it! Let me think about this for a second. Yeah! Sure! Heh heh heh. Now I remember.

BRAD PITBUHL: That's more like it. We'll go to the FBI and tell them . . . What's that sound?

KANINE BRETH: What sound?

BRAD PITBUHL: *That* sound! Don't you hear it? Is someone recording this call?

KITTY BRETH: That's for me to know and you to find out.

KANINE BRETH: Kitty! Of all the lowdown tricks!

BRAD PITBUHL: I'm outta here. You're on your own, Kanine.

KANINE BRETH: Thanks for nothing!

BRAD PITBUHL: Oh, wait. I forgot something. Kitty, are you still there?

KITTY BRETH: Maybe.

BRAD PITBUHL: Your dad told me if I ever had an occasion to speak to you both, I should read you something.

KANINE BRETH: What is it?

BRAD PITBUHL: Hold on. It's in an envelope. I'm opening it now. Hmm. It looks like a poem.

KITTY BRETH: Oh, brother. Another stupid limerick. Just read it.

BRAD PITBUHL: Okay, here goes:

> "You've come to a new battleground
> But why aren't you looking around?
> Search singly or join
> And find the rare coin.
> I've left five in all to be found!"

[Click]

O.C.S.

Ghost Writer in Residence
43 Old Cemetery Road, The Cupola
Ghastly, Illinois

November 21

Ignatius B. Grumply
43 Old Cemetery Road
Ghastly, Illinois

Dearest Iggy,

It's all my fault. I was trying to make Seymour take responsibility for his actions. Instead, I made him feel guilty for keeping a secret and scaring away Shadow. I had no right to do that. I never should've thought I could raise a child— or even a cat.

I have purchased an ad in tomorrow's newspaper in the hopes that wherever Seymour is, he's still reading the paper.

Good-bye, Iggy. I've enjoyed sharing my home with you. I hope that by leaving I can make it

71.

possible for you and Seymour to live here together happily ever after.

Love always,

Olive

P.S. Almost forgot: I found a funny little coin in front of the house. I'll leave it on the dining room table.

➤THE GHASTLY TIMES◄

Saturday, November 22
Cliff Hanger, Editor

"Your Secrets Are Our Business"

50 Cents
Morning Edition

Fourth Coin Found!

Ignatius Grumply found it on his dining room table. But he says the 1796 gold coin was discovered by Olive C. Spence, who left it for him before departing.

No matter who found it, the coin is worth $1.38 million, according to M. Balm, chief librarian at the Ghastly Public Library.

"It's known as a No Stars quarter eagle," said Balm. "It's quite rare and interesting."

"I have no interest in the coin," said Grumply, "other than in offering it as a reward for the return of my missing family."

Grumply says that this month his son, Seymour, a dog named Secret, a cat named Shadow and the ghost of Olive C. Spence have all run away from home, leaving the 64-year-old writer alone in the now deathly quiet mansion.

The 1796 No Stars quarter eagle is the fourth rare coin discovered in Ghastly in recent weeks.

Grumply offers rare coin as reward for return of missing family.

Breths Wait with Bated Breath for Reading of Will

Kanine and Kitty continue to fight like, well, cats and dogs.

As far as Kitty and Kanine Breth are concerned, tomorrow's reading of their father's last will and testament couldn't come soon enough.

"As soon as I get my millions, I'm out of here," said Kanine Breth.

"Well, I've already booked my plane ticket back to Cat Creek," said Kitty Breth. "I'll be flying first class, thanks to my inheritance."

Both Breths believe they alone will inherit their father's millions.

(Continued on page 2, column 1)

WILL *(Continued from page 1, column 2)*

"Just do the math," said Kitty Breth. "Daddy's treasures were valued at seven million dollars shortly before his death. He gave away $576,500 worth of rare books. Then he sold all of his antiques and artwork for $6,423,500. He exchanged that money for five coins, according to a limerick he gave Brad Pitbuhl to read to us. So far, four coins have been found totaling $1,423,500. That leaves one more coin worth five million dollars—for me!"

"You mean me!" growled Kanine.

One Coin Left!

"Look for the 1913 Liberty Nickel," says Librarian

Balm says Noah Breth would've been tickled by story of rare nickel.

There is only one rare coin left to be found. And M. Balm thinks he knows what it might be.

"I'd look for the 1913 Liberty nickel," says Balm, chief librarian at the Ghastly Public Library and president of the newly formed Numismatics Club of Ghastly.

The 1913 Liberty Head nickel has an interesting history. "Only five were made at the U.S. Mint," explained Balm. "Evidence suggests they were made in secret by a former employee of the Mint who later advertised that he was looking to buy the rare coin, which he in fact had made."

The 1913 Liberty Head nickel was never placed in circulation. As a result the coin has become a favorite with collectors. It's valued today at five million dollars—the exact amount that remains unaccounted for in Noah Breth's estate.

"It makes sense that Noah would put his money in a 1913 Liberty Head nickel," said Balm. "Not only was Noah born in 1913, but he loved a good story. I suspect he'd be tickled by the story of the Liberty nickel."

Balm speculated that the rare coin could turn up tomorrow when Rita O'Bitt reads Noah Breth's will. "Maybe Mr. Breth left this coin to be shared by his children," said Balm. "Or maybe he left it for someone else to discover. In any case, I advise Ghastlyians to be dogged in their search for the 1913 Liberty nickel!"

An Important Announcement

From the Creators of
43 Old Cemetery Road

November 22

Dear Subscriber:

In recent months Olive C. Spence and I have been writing a ghost story together. Our son, Seymour, provided the illustrations. Unfortunately both Olive and Seymour have run away. And because writing a book is the last thing on my mind right now, I am sending this letter to inform you that there will be no more chapters of *43 Old Cemetery Road*. Refunds will be sent as soon as I calcula

So you're throwing in the towel, are you? Too bad. I was enjoying the book.

Olive! You're back!

I'm not Olive.

Of course you are. No one else interrupts my writing like this.

The name's Breth. Noah Breth. I was a subscriber of yours. Now I'm a ghost. A ghost in training, to be precise. I'm still getting the feel for this afterlife business.

Good heavens.

So I've heard. I've not made it up that way. Still have some unfinished business here to attend to.

With your children. I've been reading about them in the newspaper.

A pair of greedy good-for-nothings. I did a lousy job raising them.

Join the club. I'm a father myself—and a terrible one at that.

I wouldn't be so sure. Maybe you're just getting the feel for it.

No, it's much worse than that. I yelled at my son. I second-guessed his mother. I drove them both to run away from home. The cat, too. And the dog.

You really are in a fine mess, aren't you?

Yes. Being in a family is tough.

Not being in a family is tougher. Remember what your life was like before you moved to Ghastly?

Of course I do. But how do you?

Funny thing happens when you become a ghost. You learn a lot about other people. And about yourself, too. Everything's much clearer from this perspective.

If it's that obvious, what should I do? I'm beginning to think I don't deserve to be a parent.

I suppose you think you sound modest with your "I don't deserve" malarkey. Well, you don't. You sound pompous and full of yourself.

And you sound like Olive.

I'd like to meet the old gal someday. She was dead by the time I was born.

And you haven't met her . . . over there?

You mean in the ghost world? No, not yet.

Then I should warn you: She's a cat person. Or I should say, a cat *ghost*.

That's how it works.

What do you mean?

It's the first thing you learn when you become a ghost. It's almost impossible to change on this side.

I'm not sure I understand.

When you're alive you take for granted the ability you have to change your mind or your behavior. You lose that when you become a ghost.

Is that why Olive seems so stubborn at times?

Maybe. Or maybe she's just frustrated with you.

With me? Why?

Because you *can* change. You can wake up every day and be a different person, just in the way you live your life. Ghosts can't do that. We're locked into the personality we had when we died. So to float by and see someone like you sitting there with that defeated look on your face . . . Well, let's just say it can be a bit off-putting, my friend.

I think I'm starting to understand.

Most people do, but usually not until the end of their lives. Then they think it's too late to make a change, even a small one. That's why I put my fortune in coins.

Oh, yes. Those rare coins turning up all over town. What's that about?

I wanted to remind people that sometimes small change can be extremely valuable.

You were a clever man.

Thank you. But I wasn't a very good father. If I could do it over again differently, I would. The point is, I don't have that chance now.

But I do.

Yes. You do.

Then if you'll excuse me, I have a son to find.

Good. And I'll try to locate your friend, Miss Spence.

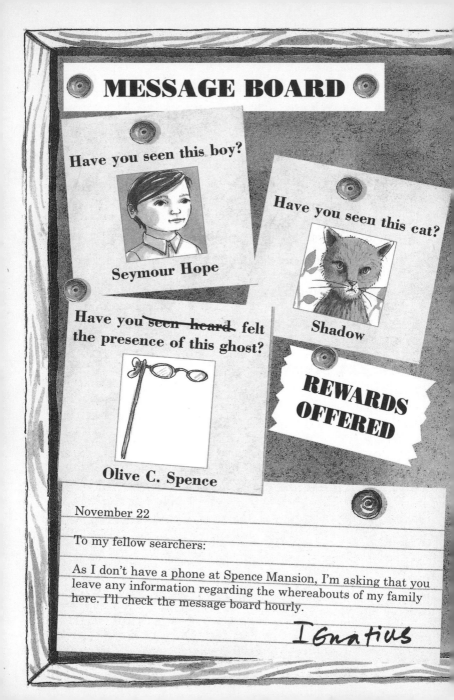

November 22

Dear Mr. Grumply,

It is with a heavy heart that I write to confess something that's been bothering me for days.

Earlier this month I paid a visit to your house to tell Seymour that Secret was Noah Breth's dog. Seymour was aware of this fact, but he asked me to keep it a secret. I agreed, thinking no harm could come from a nice boy caring for a dead man's dog. But I now see how wrong I was. I'd hate to think a family as fine as yours could be torn apart by one small secret—or one big Secret.

In brighter news, I wanted to let you know that I saw Seymour early this morning on Gruel Drive. Secret was with him. Both boy and dog looked healthy and warm. Unfortunately, when I called over to Seymour, he and Secret took off running toward Scary Street.

I'll continue to look for your son, as I know you will. In the meantime, I hope you can forgive me for keeping a secret from you.

Yours sincerely,

Rita O'Bitt

Rita O'Bitt

THE GHASTLY GOURMAND

~~◇~~ 14 Scary Street
Ghastly, Illinois ~~◇~~

November 23

Dear Ignatius,

I need to take a quick break from searching for Seymour to apologize to you.

I told Seymour weeks ago that the dog that followed him home from the library was Noah Breth's dog. Seymour already knew this, but he begged me not to tell you for fear you'd make him return the dog to the Old Breth Place.

Of course I planned to tell you anyway. (I have kids of my own!) But I got so distracted by that coin I found in the tip jar, I flat-out forgot. And now look what's happened.

Anyway, I'm writing to tell you not to worry too much. I'm pretty sure Seymour and Secret have been here the last few mornings for breakfast. I guess everybody in town knows I don't lock the front door when I'm in the kitchen cooking. From the looks of my bakery shelf and refrigerator, Seymour's been living on pumpkin muffins, brownies, and chocolate milk. Might not be the most balanced diet in town, but it won't kill him.

Don't worry, Ignatius. We'll find Seymour.

Yours in search of Hope,

Shirley U. Jest
Shirley U. Jest

➤ THE GHASTLY TIMES ◀

"Your Secrets Are Our Business"

Cliff Hanger, Editor

November 23

Dear Ignatius,

Like everyone else in town, I've been up all night looking for Seymour. When I got to work an hour ago, I found this picture from our night photographer. It was taken at the Old Breth Place.

I guess it's not surprising that Seymour would eventually take Secret back home. And dare I confess I knew all along that the dog belonged to the late Noah Breth?

I've always said that secrets are our business, but I'm beginning to rethink that. Maybe a secret that hurts somebody is as bad as a lie.

In any case, as soon as I saw this photo I went out to the Old Breth Place myself to talk to Seymour. But he wasn't there. Neither was Secret.

The only thing I found was a letter that Seymour was writing to you. I can't make heads or tails of it. Maybe you can.

Yours with no secrets,

Cliff Hanger

Cliff Hanger

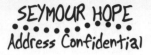

November 23

Ignatius B. Grumply
43 Old Cemetery Road
Ghastly, Illinois

Dear Mr. Grumply,

I'm really sorry I ran away, especially because I didn't get a chance to tell you something important. The reason I left had nothing to do with you or Olive. It was my fault. I wasn't a very good son.

And I wasn't a very good parent.

Olive! You found me!

Clearly I need to find a new style of writing.

Is that you, Olive?

No. The name's Breth. Noah Breth.

Oh, you're the man who . . .

Died? Yes, that's me. Don't be afraid to use the word, lad. It's perfectly natural.

You were Secret's owner, weren't you?

I preferred to say we were friends.

I like that. And I really like Secret.

Terrific dog, isn't he? An Irish wolfhound. I wouldn't have any other kind. He was my faithful companion for more than ten years.

Olive thinks he looks like a rag mop. Do you know Olive?

No, not yet. I know only that you love her, don't you?

Of course.

And what about Ignatius Grumply? You love him, too, don't you?

Yeah. But I hate myself. Why did I lie to them?

I don't deserve to be their son.

Ah, stop with that foolish talk. You made a mistake. I made plenty of them in my life. The goal isn't to be perfect.

It's not?

'Course not! Your job is to do the best you can in every circumstance.

What happens when you mess up?

Well, you learn your lesson. You make a small change. Then you try again the next day. It sounds simple, I know. But it's a grand arrangement you have there when you're living.

I never thought about it that way.

Most people don't. But as an artist, haven't you ever had to draw something a second time?

I have to draw most pictures three or four times before they're any good.

Exactly so. Now think of life in the same terms. Start over when you have to. Make a second draft. Or a third. Embrace the chance you have to do things over again in a different, better, wiser way.

I bet you're going to tell me to go home now, aren't you?

No. I have a better idea.

Really? What?

I'd like you to attend the reading of my will in Rita O'Bitt's office. Nine o'clock.

That's just fifteen minutes from now. What should I say? What should I do?

Just go. You'll know what to do when you get there.

Should I ma

No time for chatting, Seymour. Off you go!

READING OF THE
LAST WILL AND TESTAMENT
OF
NOAH BRETH

SUNDAY, NOVEMBER 23
9:00 A.M.

RITA O'BITT: Because this matter is under litigation, I have asked a court reporter to attend today's proceedings and transcribe everything that's said. Are you ready to begin?

COURT REPORTER: I am.

RITA O'BITT: Good. Then let's take a roll call so we have a record of the people in this room. Kanine Breth?

KANINE BRETH: Here.

RITA O'BITT: Kitty Breth?

KITTY BRETH: I'm here. And c'mon, let's get this show on the road. I have a plane to catch.

RITA O'BITT: All right. I am unsealing the last will of the late Noah Breth.

[Sound of envelope being torn]

KANINE BRETH: Enough with the drama already. Just tell us who gets the 1913 Liberty nickel.

RITA O'BITT: Before I do, I will note for the record that the will is written in verse.

KITTY BRETH: Of course it is. Just read it!

RITA O'BITT: Okay, here goes:

> "There once was a man with money
> Who thought of a plan quite funny
> To give his two kids
> One last little quiz
> And now it's almost all done-y."

KANINE BRETH: All *done-y?* That's awful!

KITTY BRETH: Daddy was obviously sick when he wrote that.

RITA O'BITT: May I continue?

KANINE BRETH: Go on.

RITA O'BITT: The will continues:

"I wish I'd been the kind of dad
Who raised nice kids who made him glad.
But my progeny
Didn't care for me.
What they loved was the fortune I had.

"And now that I'm practically dead
But before I'm heavy as lead
I want you to know
That most of my dough
Is hidden on a furry friend's—"

[Secret enters, barking, with Seymour Hope behind]

SEYMOUR HOPE: I'm sorry to interrupt, but I have something to tell you. Secret was your dad's dog.

[Secret barks]

KITTY BRETH: I know. So?

KANINE BRETH: What do you want us to do about it?

SEYMOUR HOPE: Well, I thought you'd want him. He was your dad's faithful companion for more than ten years.

KITTY BRETH: I don't care about that dog.
I just want the Liberty nickel.

KANINE BRETH: Me, too. Get that stinky
mutt out of here!

SEYMOUR HOPE: You really don't want him?

KITTY BRETH: No!

KANINE BRETH: Heck, no!

SEYMOUR HOPE: Great! Thanks! I'm going back
home now. I can't wait to tell Olive and
Mr. Grumply!

[Ignatius Grumply enters, hugs Seymour]

IGNATIUS GRUMPLY: Seymour! I'm so happy to
see you, son.

SEYMOUR HOPE: You're not mad at me for
running away or lying?

IGNATIUS GRUMPLY: No. I'm just glad you're
safe.

KITTY BRETH: Oh, please. Spare us the
happy endings.

KANINE BRETH: Yeah, why don't you scram,
the both of you? And take that mangy dog

with you.

IGNATIUS GRUMPLY: Forgive the intrusion. We'll get out of your hair now.

[Ignatius, Seymour, and Secret start to leave; Secret barks]

SEYMOUR HOPE: Come on, boy. Come on!

[Secret continues to bark]

IGNATIUS GRUMPLY: Seems he doesn't want to leave.

KITTY BRETH: Will you just grab the stupid dog and go? We're trying to listen to Daddy's last will and testament.

[Seymour holds Secret by the collar and pulls the dog toward the door]

SEYMOUR HOPE: Oh, no.

KANINE BRETH: Now what?

SEYMOUR HOPE: Secret's collar just broke.

KITTY BRETH: If you don't get that dog out of here right now, I'm going to—

RITA O'BITT: Wait. Stop right there. Court reporter, do you have a camera with you?

COURT REPORTER: Yes.

RITA O'BITT: Please get a picture of that small round object hanging on Secret's collar. But first let me polish it with a clean handkerchief.

⋙THE GHASTLY TIMES⋘

Sunday, November 23
Cliff Hanger, Editor

"We're Changing Our Ways!"

30 Nickels
Special Late Edition

WHATTA *COIN*-CIDENCE!

Secret's collar held the Liberty nickel.

Did Secret bark because his collar was too tight? Or because he missed his old friend, the late Noah Breth?

Or did the sofa-sized dog know that a coin valued at $5 million was hanging on his collar behind his nametag?

We might never know for sure.

"If Secret knew, he certainly lived up to his name by keeping it a secret," said Rita O'Bitt, who was as surprised as anyone when the coin was discovered this morning during the reading of Noah Breth's will.

According to O'Bitt, Breth left a riddle wrapped in a limerick for his two children, Kitty and Kanine Breth, to solve. "Noah said in his first poem that he'd 'made sense' of his wealth," explained O'Bitt. "I think that was a clever way of saying that he'd put his money into coins or *cents*. He also noted that he hid his fortune in what he treasured most on earth. Since arriving in Ghastly,

Kitty and Kanine have turned the town upside down, looking for their father's treasure. I guess they never thought it could be his dog."

O'Bitt said that a court reporter has it on record that both Kitty and Kanine Breth rejected Seymour Hope's offer to return Secret to them. "That means Seymour is now the legal owner of both Secret and the 1913 Liberty nickel," said O'Bitt.

Kitty Breth refused requests for interviews for this story. In a rare moment of solidarity, her brother did the same.

After the discovery of the coin on the collar, the reading of Noah Breth's will continued. O'Bitt said there was little new information contained in the legal document other than instructions on where Breth wanted his ashes scattered.

"Where do you think?" said O'Bitt. "County Limerick, Ireland, of course!"

Can Seymour Keep a Secret?

Hope was temporarily in the doghouse but no more.

Earlier today Seymour Hope abandoned his temporary home in Secret's old doghouse and, after a brief stop at Rita O'Bitt's law office, returned home to Spence Mansion with his father, Ignatius Grumply.

"Once I heard Kitty and Kanine didn't want their dad's dog, I knew I could go home and explain the whole thing to Olive and Mr. Grumply," said Hope.

And what did Grumply say?

"I never minded Seymour keeping the dog," Grumply insisted. "What I didn't like was my son's dishonesty. Seymour knew he should've asked the Breth children if they wanted to care for their father's dog. Now that he's done that, I'm satisfied. But there's another matter concerning Secret that I need to discuss with Seymour. It's serious."

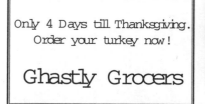
Plans for New Chapters on Hold

Readers of the serialized ghost story *43 Old Cemetery Road* should not expect three new chapters by Thanksgiving as originally promised.

"With all the recent dog excitement, combined with my cat allergies, which seem to get worse every day, there's been no time to work on the book," said Ignatius Grumply. "And with Olive gone, I don't see how we can possibly make our Thanksgiving deadline."

Olive C. Spence, a feline fan, is no longer living at Spence Mansion. Nor is the cat, Shadow, said Grumply with a sneeze. "I can't for the life of me figure out why my cat allergies are still bothering me if the darn cat isn't even here," he added.

Grumply said that he plans to send subscribers a letter explaining the situation and offering full refunds.

New chapters are the last thing on Grumply's mind.

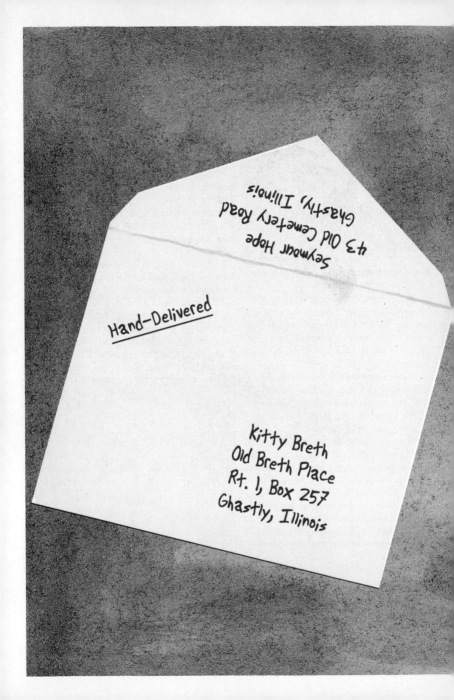

Seymour Hope
43 Old Cemetery Road
Ghastly, Illinois

Hand-Delivered

Kitty Breth
Old Breth Place
Rt. 1, Box 257
Ghastly, Illinois

Seymour Hope
43 Old Cemetery Road
Ghastly, Illinois

Hand-Delivered

Kanine Breth
Old Breth Place
Rt. 1, Box 257
Ghastly, Illinois

SEYMOUR R HOPE
• • • • • • • • • • • •
Illustrator in Residence

43 Old Cemetery Road
Third Floor
Ghastly, Illinois

November 24

Kitty and Kanine Breth
Rt. 1, Box 257
Ghastly, Illinois

Dear Kitty and Kanine,

You can have the 1913 Liberty nickel. I don't want
it. I just want Secret. He's the best dog I've ever
had. To be honest, he's the only dog I've ever had.
I like Shadow, too, of course. But cats don't like
to play the way dogs do.

The only thing better than having a dog would be
to have a brother or sister. I'd give anything for

that. I know you two fight a lot. But if you ever sat down and really thought about it, you'd realize how lucky you are to have someone to talk to and play with. Someone to teach you how to throw a curveball or turn a cartwheel. Someone to tell your secrets to.

Having a dog is nice, too. Just not as nice as having a brother or sister.

I'm going to sign this letter now and tear it in half. That way you two will have to get together to read it.

Sincerely,

    -Seymour

P.S. Let me know when I should deliver the coin to you.

P.P.S. Your dad was really cool.

Kitty Breth

Route 1, Box 257
Ghastly, Illinois

<u>Delivered in Person</u>

November 24

Seymour Hope
43 Old Cemetery Road
Ghastly, Illinois

Dear Seymour,

You are a very generous boy. And a wise one, too. But strangely enough, after searching high and low for Daddy's money, I find that's not what I want after all.

I was mortified to learn that Daddy considered his dog to be his most valuable treasure. But it's true. I was a terrible daughter. I rarely visited or called him. And I never wrote letters to him, except when I needed money.

Now that Daddy's dead, there's nothing I can do about that. But I can try to be a better sister and a nicer person. That's what I want more than any coin in the world.

So please give the 1913 Liberty nickel to Kanine. Tell him I'm sorry for being such a selfish, sneaky sister. And if it's not too much trouble, would you mind bringing Secret over sometime to visit? I canceled my plane ticket back to Montana. I'd like to stick around for a while and get to know the people—and the dog—who knew and loved my dad best.

Sincerely,

Kitty Breth

Kitty Breth

P.S. I'm too old to be your sister, but if ever you're looking to adopt an aunt, I'd like to apply for the position.

November 24

Seymour Hope
43 Old Cemetery Road
Ghastly, Illinois

Dear Seymour,

I was a rotten son and a miserable brother. I never thought about anyone except myself.

I'd like to change that, beginning with the 1913 Liberty nickel. Please give it to Kitty. It's the least I can do to apologize for my cruddy behavior.

Also, I know I told you that I didn't want Secret. And you have every right to keep the dog for yourself. But if you wouldn't mind bringing him by the house sometime to visit, I'd really appreciate it.

I'm planning to stay in Ghastly for a while to get my life straightened out. I don't think I could turn a cartwheel to save my life, but I did throw a pretty mean curveball back in high school. I'd be happy to teach you how.

Hope to see you soon.

Sincerely,

Kanine Breth

Kanine Breth

P.S. This is the first nice letter I've ever written. And it wasn't even that hard. Fact is, it was kinda fun. Guess my old dad was smarter than I thought.

43 Old Cemetery Road
Third Floor
Ghastly, Illinois

November 24

Hey, Mr. Grumply!

Will you take a look at these letters I got from Kitty and Kanine Breth? What should I do?

Also, what's the serious matter you wanted to talk to me about?

     —Seymour

P.S. It's nice to be home.

IGNATIUS B. GRUMPLY

A WRITER IN RESIDENCE

43 OLD CEMETERY ROAD   2ND FLOOR   GHASTLY, ILLINOIS

November 24

Seymour Hope
Third floor
43 Old Cemetery Road
Ghastly, Illinois

Dear Seymour,

It's nicer to have you home, son. I missed you.

We do have several matters to discuss. First, on the business front, I've written a letter to subscribers outlining a refund program. Would you please help me address and stuff envelopes? I'd like to get them in the mail today.

Second, in regard to Secret, this was my mistake more than yours. We need to be more sensitive to Olive. She made it clear from the start that she was a cat person. We take for granted the chance we have—the gift, really—of waking up each day and being a different person on account of our actions. Olive can't do that. As a ghost, it's very difficult for her to change. Even if she wanted to become a dog person—or a dog ghost—I don't think she could.

It appears from the letters you received from Kitty and Kanine that they're regretting their decision to give away Secret. So I think you should return the dog to the Breths, for their sakes as well as Olive's. There's no need to tell them why you're doin

Now look who's being a sneak.

Olive! You're back.

I am.

I'm glad. But you have no right to read my personal correspondence. And please note that I'm not shouting or barking at you. I'm simply stating a fact.

I know, dear. But now can you understand why I act the way I do? I can't help myself. So carry on with your letter.

Olive, you really *can* be maddening at times.

But you love me anyway.

I do love you. And you're going to love me right back after Seymour returns Secret to the Old Breth Place. Seems Seymour has inspired the bad Breths to be good for a change.

What a lovely surprise! In return, I have a surprise for Seymour. Look out the window.

Is that what I think it is?

Isn't he precious?

But Olive, you despise dogs.

That's not a dog. It's a puppy.

Do you know what puppies grow up to be?

I'll slink over that bridge when I come to it.

You never cease to amaze me.

As a very wise ghost once said, sometimes small change can be extremely valuable.

Noah Breth said that! Olive, were you eavesdropping on us?

I'm sorry, Iggy. Old habits die hard.

But why couldn't Noah see you?

Mr. Breth is still a novice ghost. He'll learn with time and practice.

I'm sighing—heavily.

I know, dear. I'm right here.

May I finish my letter to Seymour?

Be my guest.

Well, son, disregard much of what I was writing above. I guess I'm the one who needs to make a few small changes. And I'd like to start by delivering this news to you in person. That's one of the changes I'm going to make around here. Writing letters is fine, and you must continue to write letters to your mother. But for those of us lucky to be alive, there are some things that should be said face to face. By the time you read these words, I will have told you what's been on my mind for some time now. I'll be eager to hear your thoughts on the matter.

Fondly,

Ignatius

Ignatius

P.S. What are you going to name your puppy?

43 Old Cemetery Road
Third Floor
Ghastly, Illinois

November 24

Dear Mr. Grumply—and Olive, too, because I'm sure you're reading over his shoulder,

I can't tell you how much I love this puppy! Thank you, thank you, THANK YOU! I'm going to call him Willie because I never would've gotten him if it hadn't been for Noah Breth's will.

And Mr. Grumply, thanks for suggesting I start calling you Dad. But I had a dad once, remember? That didn't work out so well. I was thinking maybe I could combine Mr. Grumply and Dad and call you Mr. Dumply. But that doesn't sound very nice. Then I thought I could combine them the other way and call you Mr. Grad. But then people might think you're my grand-father.

Would you mind if I just call you Iggy, like Olive does? It's a good name and it fits you well. And Olive, when I write letters to you, I'd like to keep calling you Olive, if that's okay.

I'll return Secret to the Breths today. Oh, and about the refund program. Forget that. I have an idea for the Liberty nickel and the next three chapters of our book. Take a look at the invitation I designed, and tell me if you like the plan.

Love,

—Seymour

and Willie

O.C.S.

Ghost Writer in Residence
43 Old Cemetery Road, The Cupola
Ghastly, Illinois

November 24

Seymour,

You're brilliant! I'll start planning the menu now.

Olive

IGNATIUS B. GRUMPLY
A WRITER IN RESIDENCE

43 OLD CEMETERY ROAD　　　**2ND FLOOR**　　　**GHASTLY, ILLINOIS**

November 24

Seymour,

Leave it to you to think up the perfect solution. I'm stuffing envelopes as I write.

Iggy

You're Invited
to Celebrate the Life
of
Noah Breth

Date: Thursday, November 27
Time: 5 o'clock in the evening
Location: Spence Mansion

We're having a great big to-do,
The purpose of which is to:
Remember a friend
Whose life came to an end
And to whom we say "IOU!"

After the celebration, guests will be treated to
a reading of the next three chapters of
43 Old Cemetery Road and a grand Thanksgiving feast.

Please bring an appetite and a healthy sense of humor!

Note: All travel expenses will be paid by the creators
of 43 Old Cemetery Road. Free lodging is available at
the Old Breth Place,
compliments of Kitty and Kanine Breth.

Friday, November 28
Cliff Hanger, Editor

"Why Not Make a Small Change?"

50 Cents
Morning Edition

A Funeral in Rhyme
and They All Had a Good Time!

**Breth's funeral is a mixture of
wit and wisdom.**

**Kitty and Kanine Breth
remember their father.**

Most subscribers to *43 Old Cemetery Road,* a serialized ghost story, weren't sure what to make of the invitation they received by mail earlier this week.

"I was afraid they were going to pull the plug on the book," said M. Balm, a devoted fan. "I thought this might be the end of the story."

Indeed not, said coauthor Ignatius B. Grumply.

"It's true I haven't had much time to work on the book these last few weeks," said Grumply. "But my son, Seymour, had the terrific idea of sharing with readers the

true story of a ghost we've recently met. His name is Noah Breth."

Mr. Breth died on November 3 at the age of 95. Shortly before his death Breth converted his fortune into five coins, which he scattered around Ghastly. He hid the most valuable coin, a 1913 Liberty Head nickel, on his dog's collar.

"I sold the coin and used the money to bring all of our readers from around the world together," explained Seymour Hope. "We wanted to throw a big party to celebrate what a cool guy Noah Breth was as a

(Continued on page 2, column 1)

FUNERAL *(Continued from page 1, column 2)*

person and what a great ghost he's going to be."

In honor of Breth's Irish ancestry, the funeral celebration included songs, funny stories, much laughter and plenty of limericks. Grumply and Spence wrote their tribute to Breth in a series of five-line poems. Seymour Hope illustrated the limericks in a program that was distributed to guests.

But didn't Breth leave instructions with attorney Rita O'Bitt specifying that he didn't want a funeral?

"He did," confirmed O'Bitt. "But I don't think even Noah could've envisioned a funeral like this. Keep in mind that he said if people wanted to do something in his honor, they should do whatever makes them smile."

Perhaps the most surprising smiles at Breth's funeral were those of his two children.

"I feel like for the first time in my life I'm really getting to know Daddy," said Kitty.

"Me, too," said Kanine. "I wish he could've seen Kitty and me getting along so well."

Both Kitty and Kanine Breth have decided to remain at the Old Breth Place for now. "My sister and I have a lot of catching up to do," said Kanine.

Look Who Has a New Dog (But Willie Bark?)

Even before Seymour Hope had a chance to return Secret to the Old Breth Place, he had a new canine cohort, Willie.

"Isn't he great?" asked Hope. "He's an Irish wolfhound, just like Secret."

Secret, former companion to Noah Breth, is back at his old house with Kitty and Kanine Breth.

"We're so grateful to Seymour for letting us take care of Dad's treasured friend," said Kitty Breth.

Hope said he's the one who should be grateful. "If it hadn't been for Secret, I never would've met Noah Breth. He gave me some really good advice that I will treasure forever."

Seymour hopes his new dog will be less vocal than Secret.

Shadow Had a Secret, Too

Shadow introduces her new kittens.

No wonder Ignatius Grumply was sneezing so much.

Shadow, the resident feline at 43 Old Cemetery Rd., didn't run away from Spence Mansion after all. The cat had simply retreated under Grumply's bed to have her—yes, *her*—kittens.

"Mother and babies are doing fine," said Grumply, who suffers from severe cat allergies.

Shadow's secret was revealed during Noah Breth's funeral, when the cat and kittens joined the celebration.

"I always thought Shadow was a male cat," admitted Grumply.

"I did, too," said Seymour Hope.

Hope promised Grumply that he would feed and care for the new kittens, as well as Shadow and Willie.

Grumply promised his housemates that he would make an appointment with an allergist immediately.

The End

(for now)

ACKNOWLEDGMENTS

Thanks
to our
feline friends
and
canine comrades
for their
*paws*itively
*purr*fect
contribution
to this story
and
to our lives.

Aldo

Cooper

Butterfly

China

Forty

How to Write a Limerick

I hope that I shall have the time
To write my will in verse and rhyme.
  "To friends in good health
  I leave all my wealth."
Now how shall I split this half dime?